Finding Pig Man

A Horror Novella

By Thomas Stewart

Thomas Stewart

Published independently by Thomas Stewart in the United States of America

First Printing, 2023

1226 White Ln. Gastonia, N.C. 28052
Email: thomasxdrwho@gmail.com
Phone: (980) 289 - 2126

For David, the man that made me for so long believe in the existence of "Pig Man".

God rest, buddy

1

When we're young, we tend to latch onto things that grown ups tell us, even when we really shouldn't. We tend to have an imagination that makes us believe things that we wouldn't otherwise if we were more mature. Sometimes it's to bond with us, sometimes it's to keep us in line, and then sometimes, well...

Well sometimes it's to enlighten us.

"The world's a cruel place," my old man always used to tell me, "full of strange and unusual things." I never understood what he would've meant by that and anytime I tried asking, he wouldn't say anything other than, "Just keep your head down and your rear lower, okay little buddy?" He always kept this mystic, ominous sort of look about him whenever he'd tell me these things, too. These conversations, naturally, tended to be brief and few and far between. Every time, though, it would always be kicked up by one topic: "Pig Man".

Now, to explain in the simplest way possible, "Pig Man" is exactly what he sounds like; a big ass mutant pig that walks on two legs. How he got that way or where the hell he came from, now that's a lot trickier a question, one that, even after all that happened, I still for the life of me can't give you an answer for. God knew the old man, rest his soul, couldn't either, and nor could any of the other ten or twelve people that used to always tell me about him growing up.

It was never clear on who ever saw him first, where, or when, but I can tell you that the last time he was seen, it was somewhere in the mountains up near the peak. "Pig Man" has supposedly been implicated in the deaths of at least five people, two of which were State Troopers. Now, I'm sure you can already hear the "Those that venture up that mountain NEVER RETURN, MWA-HA-HA" speeches (accompanied by the cartoonish pipe organs and thunderclap, of course) that were constantly spewed at me by just about every bumpkin in my small little town in North Carolina, can't you?

Like I said, young and impressionable, just like anyone else here. Thing was, you know how with most ghost stories like this, folktales passed around small towns like this, people would usually stop trying to spook you once you hit a certain age? You'd reach about 13, 14, maybe 15 at the latest, and people would finally decide that you're too old to be being scared of "The Pig Man"? Well, apparently my town didn't get that memo because I can remember right up to the point where the incident began, hearing some sort of story or superstition about "Pig Man" or the mountain being "Cursed by his spirit" or something along those lines.

The legends were obviously inconsistent as hell, too. In some stories, he's just an overgrown pig monster like I said before, while in others, he's more like this pig god, able to manipulate the minds of people he sees, and some even say that he can possess their bodies and turn them into pig people. The legends may have varied in terms of what he could and couldn't do, but a couple key things would remain the same, aside from his appearance, obviously. For starters, "Pig Man" sightings were always set in the mountains, and usually in a dense forested area.

Another thing is that there were never any survivors, which of course meant that there weren't any photos of him, either. Because of this, also, yes, that meant that, at least to anyone outside our town, there was no proof that it was him or that he even existed. The one and only time, like I said before, was back in, I think the mid 50s-early 60s, when a guy and his wife camped out up near the mountaintop one night and supposedly was attacked by "Pig Man", which he was the sole survivor of.

Again, no photos or anything of the creature were taken, and thanks to the fact that the two were your real redneck types, people who think that they're "Gettin' away from 'The Man'" by squatting in the mountains, the guy's testimony was laughable, to put it kindly. It didn't help either that he was high off his ass when it happened as well, which did bring up the possibility that he'd killed his wife, possibly from a mental or drug induced breakdown. Either way, the result in the end was that he was sentenced to psychiatric care after being deemed mentally unfit to stand trial, and the wife's body was never found because no one in my town dared setting foot on the mountain.

Until the day he died, alone in the hospital, he kept to his story, that "Pig Man" had abducted his wife and butchered her right in front of his eyes on the mountain that night. Everyone in town believed him, too, down to the last detail. I, of course, was one of those people, even when I grew up and started looking past fantasy and keeping myself down to earth, I never doubted the man's story, at least to an extent. Looking back, at least from what I could find of his testimonies, he never embellished his experience like you might expect. Like he never claimed to have to fight off "Pig Man" or trick him or anything to get away. In fact, he himself always claimed that he never knew exactly how or why he was allowed to live.

According to him, he watched his wife get brutally murdered by "Pig Man", and then he heard squeals from all around the campsite before he blacked out and when he woke up, he was at the base of the mountain with only the memory of his wife's murder from the previous night. I guess, to me, it reads like how you'd read or hear about other cryptid or paranormal encounters; stuff like blacking out after a traumatic experience, losing time and memory, and perhaps even an induction of madness or insanity following it. Of course, like I'd mentioned before, there were plenty of things that negated anything related to the paranormal and suggested something much more grounded, more psychological, such as the guy having lost his mind and his temper, thanks to a drug induced hysteria, and went berserk on his wife, imagining the whole time that a giant monster pig was doing it the entire time.

I always believed the former though, like everybody else, and it was the tail end of last month when I decided to prove it for myself. I was in town for a family get together, namely my old man's 59th birthday, and I came across a missing persons poster taped to the boarded up window of the old corner store just down the road from my house. I remember how I used to see a whole bunch of them back in the day, usually teenagers or college kids, getting lost after making a trip up there for spring break or some shit. This one was of a 15 year old Amelia Hill. According to the poster, she was last seen about a month before, going up the mountain on a camping trip with her father.

Now, I can't really tell you why exactly, not even now, but something about the way she looked, just how young she looked, got to me. Well, I take that back, maybe I can, in a way. I feel like when I saw that photo, I was reminded of my step-sister. Bonnie was kidnapped at around that age, 16 to be exact, and she hasn't been found to this day. Of course, that was a much different case. We all knew who did it. Her piece of goatshit father had been harassing both my mother and father for weeks leading up to her disappearance. The cops knew he did it, the town knew he did it, and we sure as hell knew he did it, but when they managed to find his ass, no one could get him to sing, which meant there was no location of her.

Thing was, I had actually spoken to her on the phone that day she went missing. I was on the way to pick her up from the mall, but when I got there, well... No Bonnie. I'm telling you this to say that Amelia reminded me of Bonnie, and therefore reminded me of the guilt that's haunted me for years ever since. I saw the picture of Amelia and I saw Bonnie crying out, asking me why I couldn't have been there for her. In short, although I never met this little girl, I couldn't help but take this personally.

I took the poster off the window and pocketed it. When I got to my old childhood home, and after chumming it up with the folks for a while, you know, I managed to get Dad alone and showed him the poster. "Where'd you find this, son?" he asked me.

"The old corner store."

"Oh, he he, that old place." He chuckled dryly. "Yeah, bout all that old place is good for these days anyway, ain't it; a billboard."

"Have you ever seen the girl before though?" I asked, trying not to push too hard. Like I said, these things had always been a sort of sore subject with him. He shook his head.

"Not personally, I mean, sure I've heard talk of a coupla people goin' missing' after hiking their dumb asses up there, but that just goes to show ya, people can't never take a man at his word. When they tell ya "Don't do this" or "Don't go there", it might be wise to pay attention to 'em, don't you agree, Roy?"

"I guess so." I sighed. "Still though, don't you think eventually someone should maybe try and--"

"What, so they can get screwed sideways too?" He barked a snide laugh at me. "God, son, what've they been fillin' your head with up at uni, huh? You been hitting up too many of them parties, ain't ya?"

"No dad, it's not like that, it's just... Just..." I trailed off. I couldn't think of anything to say, nothing that'd convince him anymore. "I don't know, don't worry about it." I got up and was about to walk away when dad called for me to stop. I did and turned around again to see him getting up to come to me.

"Everything going okay?" He fixed me in his trademark "Be straight with me" stare.

"Yeah."

"Everything still going okay with your classes?"

"Yeah, yeah, everything's fine with me and all, it's just..." I sighed again. "Let me ask you something, dad, do you still have nightmares, about Bonnie I mean?" His eyes fell to the ground.

"Only every night." he replied in a gravelly, somber voice. He sighed and then said, "Roy, I'd sell my goddamned soul just to have her home again. Hell, Lord himself knows Ashley would've too." He looked up at the sky. For a brief second, I thought I could see tears welling up in his eyes.

"I'm... I'm sorry, Dad, I wasn't trying to bring up old memories, but... But damn it, dad, when I look at that picture, I see her, you understand? I look at this picture, and I see a helpless little girl who may or may not still be alive, you know? I just think somebody should at least try to go looking for her. I mean, what about her family, think maybe they'd want someone to try and find their daughter the way they did with Bonnie?"

"Son, I've always admired how your head's been screwed on straight through the years. Hell, you've kept it on better than mine was at your age, and I've always appreciated the fact that you've always had a big heart for people. Again, something you didn't get from me. But for all of that, I guess you were bound to want to think of something foolish one day or another."

"What do you mean? I just think that someone should--"

"I ain't stupid, Roy." he said, narrowing his eyes at me. "Foolish maybe, but not stupid. I know you say "somebody", but you're actually talking about yourself. You're planning on going on some crusade over this little girl, who likely ain't even alive no more -- and honestly, God help her if she is -- and for what? Because of Bonnie?"

I sighed, defeated. "Why do you think that's gonna make a difference? What, you think it's gonna clear your conscience or something, for God's sake, it wasn't your fault?"

"Wasn't it?" I asked, my own voice now breaking.

"What do you mean? Of course it wasn't. You didn't kidnap her?"

"No, I just couldn't be there to save her, that's all."

"Roy, you can't do this to yourself, son." he said in his gravelly voice again. sighing, he said to me, "Look, I know you miss your sister. I wish she could've been found too, okay, trust me and believe." He looked down at his half empty can of Budweiser and said, "There's plenty of nights where that little guy right there was the only thing that kept me from doing myself in. But you can't go letting guilt screw around with your head like that, you hear?"

He came up and wrapped his arms tightly around me. "I love you, son, okay? You hear me, I love you, and you're all I've got now after your mother passed. So for the love of God, please, use that sense of yours and don't go chasing things that weren't meant to be chased." He squeezed me harder and said, "Promise?"

I squeezed him back and said, "I hear ya, old man."

"Good. Good man." We let go of each other and he went back to his seat and reached around in the cooler. "Here, have a beer."

"I'll pass, but thank you." His stare looked serious again and he insisted again that I take the beer, telling me it'd "Take the edge off". I sighed and took the beer, throwing my head back and downing the shitty beer. I couldn't help but to gag on it, which just made the old man chuckle.

"Never could hold your Bud, huh, boy?" he teased. I flipped him the bird before turning and walking back into the house to get my coat to leave. My cousin, Stacy, was in the kitchen, doing dishes when I walked in. My coat was hanging on the chair behind her.

"Leaving already?" she asked.

"Yeah... Gotta... Gotta head home." I chuckled, obviously having no reason to do so. It wasn't lost on her, either.

"You okay, Roy?"

"Huh? Oh, uh... Yeah, no, I'm fine. Just need to get going before it gets dark, you know?"

"You know you can bunk over, right? Hell, it'd make Uncle Travis out there happy, right?" I scoffed.

Only about as happy as a bad memory.

"That's nice and all, but uh, yeah, I really gotta get going."

"Oh, okay." Her voice hid the disappointment a little bit better than mine did trying to hide the anxiety, but it wasn't perfect, I could still hear it. "Well here..." She sat down the plates she was washing and went over to the table and began gathering the leftover food onto a plate. "Take some of this with you, huh? Save me the trouble of trying to fit all this shit in the fridge later." She chuckled.

I said nothing. She scrounged together a plate full of the turkey, mashed potatoes, and tater tots that were left. "I'd have given you some of the cookies, too, but uh... well..." She nodded her head in the direction of Dad outside and snickered. I snickered too. The old man always had a sweet tooth rivaling Santa Claus.

She handed me the plate. "Roy, seriously though, what's going on? This whole time, you've been off lately."

"What do you mean?"

"Well, you used to be a lot more lively at these sorts of things. But ever since you got here, you've hardly said anything to any of us. And ever since you came back in from talking to Uncle Travis, you've gotten this sort of cloud hanging over your head." She narrowed her eyes on mine. "There's something bothering you, I can see it. Something you're not telling me."

I swallowed. I really just wanted to snatch the coat and leave, but she was blocking the exit. Once more as well, I underestimated her skills of observance because she shook her head, saying, "Uh, uh, uh, don't even try it. You might've gotten a little bigger than you were back in the day, but I can still take you on a one-way express to pain-town." She held her balled up fist up to me. "And you forget, my husband's a cop, you think he hasn't shown me interrogation techniques?"

I held up my hands, sighing. "Alright, alright. Look, when I came into town, I passed by the old corner store; you know, the one you, me, and Steve always used to go to every afternoon for the $0.99 Cokes and MoonPies?" She nodded. "Well, I passed it and the windows were covered with missing posters and well..."

"One of 'em stuck out, huh?"

"In a word, yeah."

"So what's got you all tangled up about it? Someone you know?" I shook my head.

"No... No, it's not that she's someone I actually know, but instead, well... It's because she reminds me of someone I do." I sighed and in a voice that was on the verge of snapping in half like a twig, I shuddered, "Bonnie." Her face sunk and she pulled me in for a hug.

"I'm sorry, Roy, I..." I held up my hand.

"It's fine, just, this little girl's been missing for a while now and well... I don't know, I just feel like someone should be out there looking for her, you know?" I took the poster out and unfolded it. "I showed this to Dad and he almost went crazy when I told him this." Stacy leaned in closer to look at the poster.

"Oh, I'll bet." she said. "Last seen headin' up the mountain", huh?" She sighed regretfully. "So I take it you're wanting to go looking for her, aren't you?" I gave her an awkward grin. She scoffed.

"That was the plan, anyway, sort of." I shrugged and took my coat. While putting it on, I said, "But, eh... I promised the old man I'd leave well enough alone."

"And?" she asked with a snide sort of grin.

"And what?"

"And since when's that ever stopped you and I from doing stupid shit before, huh?" Call me "slow", but it actually took me a second to catch on to what she was suggesting here. When I did, I almost dropped of an instant heart attack. Instinctively, her sly little smile grew.

"No!" I barked, almost shouting. "Absolutely not."

"What, you ain't scared, are you?" She giggled again.

"No, but..."

"But what, chicken?" She started squawking like a chicken.

"But I promised the old man I wouldn't." I paused for a moment after saying that. Deja Vu hit my ass like a moving train and I started laughing. Oh, the irony.

She laughed too, probably realizing the same damn thing. "I repeat my question; when has you "promising the old man" gotten in the way of us doing something dumb, huh?"

"Okay, but back then we were kids, okay? Plus, you know, we never did something like going up the mountain--"

"Even better then. Something we can cross off our list."

"Stacy, I'm serious. I don't think this's a good idea." She sighed, throwing up her hand.

"Fine, fine... Just trying to help. Maybe have a little fun with ya, you know?" I sighed.

"I know, just... I don't know, I feel like... I mean, I want to help this little girl, you know? But at the same time..." I looked out the window. "I feel like there's a reason why everybody that goes up there, like her, always ends up going missing, you know what I mean?"

"Oh, I know." she said, smiling. "Hell, I used to hear the stories of "Pig Man" too." I grinned.

"You mean the ones I used to make you piss the bed at night with?" She chuckled, flipping me the bird. I laughed too. When things settled down again, it was almost a full minute of blissful silence before reality brought us both crashing back down to the matter at hand. She still wore her sly grin.

"So... Whaddya say? Wanna go monster huntin'?" I pinched the bridge of my nose and groaned. She started tugging on my shirtsleeve. "Come on, it'll be fun, Cousin..." she pleaded, using that exact same mischievous little girl voice she did back then when she wanted us to do something we weren't supposed to.

I sighed in defeat and said, in my own childish voice, "Fine... But we can't let the old man find out." She smiled and punched me playfully in the shoulder before turning and heading out the door. I threw on my coat and followed after her. With each step, one question kept repeating over and over again; Am I doing the right thing here? What if she's gone? Is there really a "Pig Man"?

I made it all the way back to my car and she came around to the passenger side. I remember looking at her confused for five seconds like "What the hell are you doing?" She rapped on the window so I rolled it down.

"You uh... gonna give me a lift, or you expecting me to hitchhike all the way up to the mountain?"

"But... You have a car..."

"And?"

"So why're you wanting to ride shotgun with me?"

"Oh okay, so I have to go driving all by myself up the big, scary mountain; all alone, ripe for the picking for "Pig Man", is that it?"

"I mean, this was your idea."

"Was it?" I frowned.

"What do you mean, "Was it"? Yes, it was. You were the one wanting to go up the mountain."

"Because you, mister, wanted to find a little girl. And you're about to make little ol' me go up alone?" I gave her the trademark "Are you shitting me right now" look. She replied with growing puppy eyes. I'll admit, I wasn't sure whether I was supposed to laugh my ass off, tell her to hit the bricks in her own car, or relent but in the end, the winner was option 3. I rolled my eyes and opened the door for her.

"Yay, this's gonna be so much fun, ain't it cousin?" I chuckled dryly.

Yeah okay, this'll be fun. About as fun as signing a death warrant for yourself can get.

I looked back to the house one last time. The old goat was already passed out, empty beer bottles and all, scattered around him. I had to smirk at this. Classic Dad.

I remember taking another look at Stacy, then at the mountain ahead and thinking to myself, somewhat grimly, some things don't change at all. I put the car in drive and slowly drove off. By then, the sun was already gone almost completely. If there was any light from the sun left to light the roads with, the trees basically canceled it out anyway, which meant that I had to put on the high beams just to see the first three feet in front of my station wagon.

"I wonder what he'll look like." Stacy piped up finally after having spent the first 20 or so minutes in silence.

"Huh? Who?"

"'Pig Man'." I scoffed.

"Well uh... Let's think here..." I started scratching my chin like I was thinking with my right hand while keeping the other on the wheel. "Now I'm no zoologist or anything, but if I could take a guess, I'm gonna say a big ass pig that walks on two legs." She snickered. So did I. My wit amuses even myself sometimes.

"Smartass, I mean like how tall is he, you know, or maybe is he muscular or is he a lardass?"

"Hell if I'd know, Stace. Not like I've actually seen the fucker before." She snickered again. And if at all possible, I'd like to keep it this way...

I pulled off to the left into a convenience store. "Why are we stopping?" asked Stacy.

"Just stay in here for a sec, I'm gonna grab some snacks or something, you want anything?" This time, she was the confused one.

"Um... Roy, we have leftovers here in the car..."

"AND?" I retorted, mocking her voice the best I could.

"And so what're you wanting out of this place?"

"Look, I'm just gonna grab something and come back to put gas in the car, just stay here for a minute, okay?"

"O-O-Okay...?" I got out and ran inside. At the counter was an old, exhausted looking roughneck who gave me the thousand-yard stare like somehow I had done or said something that was giving him flashbacks or something like that.

"Hey uh... I'd like to uh, put $40 on 10." I cautiously placed a bag of BBQ chips and a Coke on the counter. He rang up my stuff and typed on the keyboard before telling me, in so low and grumbled a voice that I almost didn't hear him speaking, or even speaking English, that my total was $45.97. I was taking out my wallet when something caught my eye.

Behind the guy on the other end of the counter was another missing poster. This one was of another young girl, one whose name I couldn't see, thanks to the way it was all bunched up. Behind this one was a bunch of others; at least ten, maybe as much as 15 or 20. They were all crumpled up against each other, looking as if they were cluttering up a filing cabinet to the point where it wouldn't shut anymore. I must have zoned out because the next thing I knew, I was waking from semi-stupor to the cashier grunting at me.

"You plannin' on payin' for all that?" he asked, just barely more audible than last time.

"Huh? Oh uh, yeah... Yeah, sorry about that." I took my card out and as I was paying, my eyes diverted themselves back to the posters. Judging from just how old, how wrinkly and even torn a few of them looked, I didn't need to see the dates on the posters to know that some of those unfortunate little bastards have been gone quite a while, far longer than the one I was looking for.

How much anyone wanna bet THEY'RE not around anymore? The cashier impatiently woke me from another stupor by alerting me that I could actually take my damn card out of the machine and that my shit was paid for (more or less quoting him verbatim, by the way). I gritted my teeth and said "Thanks" before backing away. Of course, for some reason, my mind seemed to want to keep fixing itself on the posters.

"There somethin' funny you're seein', boy?" he asked, staring cock-eyed at me. I took a deep breath.

"No uh... Sorry, no, it's just... Those posters." I pointed to the far end of the counter. He turned to look for a second, then looked back at me.

"What about 'em?"

"Well no, I just... I was just wondering, how long have they been uh..." His eyebrow raised. My mouth articulated like I wanted to ask him something, but God forbid anything actually come out.

"Been what?" he asked.

"You know... Missing?" He looked briefly at the posters, and then back at me.

"What's it to ya?"

I took a deep breath and said, "Look, there's a little girl that went missing around here just a month ago and--" He cut me off with a barking laugh.

"Oh God, don't tell me, you're about to go pokin' around up there to look for her, right?" I shrank down a little once again. Any sort of courage I'd mustered up a second ago once again evaporated. He busted up laughing again. His rotund belly bounced like it was a trampoline with each guffaw. I sighed, gritting my teeth, balling up my fist, while simultaneously holding in every urge to not lunge at this fat fuck and lodge my fist in his bottom jaw (Seriously, he was laughing at the fact that KIDS WERE MISSING, what the fuck?!).

Instead, I forced the most painfully plastic smile on my face and said, "Yes sir, I do, and I personally don't see what's so wrong about that, unless of course you're trying to tell me you know something about why they're gone... Something you don't want the cops knowing." As soon as I said this, he immediately shut up.

"What you mean, "Somethin' I don't want the cops knowin"?"

"Like maybe where the bodies are?" I said this with such pride, too. His eyes bulged. I started shrinking down a bit again. The way he was looking in that instant, I was sure hillbilly Jim here was about to jump across the fuckin' counter at me. He was shaking violently, too, which made me prone to turning and gunning it out of the place and back to the car.

About five seconds passed with nothing happening, save for the two of us staring each other down with an aura of pure anxiety spiking around us with each one. "Y-You think... I did somethin'... t-to those kids?!" he asked, his voice shaking almost as much as his body was. I said nothing. My body twitched, trying to force me to the door. "Huh? Do you?!"

"A-A-All I was trying to do was ask what happened to--" I was silenced by him slamming his wooden club of a fist on the counter, actually creating a dent in it.

"You scrawny little spit-fuck! You have no idea what I'd give to have been able to help kids like that!"

"I-I'm s-sor--"

"Oh I'll bet you are. Scroungy little shit, I'll bet you are "sorry". You know what, I'm sorry too, sorry you don't have enough sense not to ask bullshitty questions when you don't know squat yourself." Another two seconds passed like they had before, with me just trying to ready myself for this guy to come across the counter at me, before he eventually settled back down and shrank behind the counter again.

I opened my mouth to speak, or rather to apologize, but he actually beat me to it. "I... I'm sorry..." he said, in a much more somber tone this time than before. "I just... nobody's ever asked me about them before." he looked at the posters again. "Look son... I... I..." He trailed off, not taking his eyes away from the poster.

"You lost someone?" I asked. Honestly, I don't know how or why I made this assumption, but it turned out to be true anyway because he nodded. He sighed, wiping his eyes. "H-How long ago?"

"Years." he said in a gravelly voice. I could hear him sniffing. My heart began to melt. I couldn't help it, I mean, just a few seconds ago, he was ready to break my scrawny ass in half and now he was crumbling at my feet.

"Hey uh... M-Maybe you should..."

"What, seek a therapist, talk to someone about it? Yeah, thanks, I already tried that."

"I was actually gonna say you should come with me. Maybe we could--"

"Nuh-uh." he said, shaking his head. I could see his eyes welling up now, too. "It... It wouldn't do 'em any good."

"Why not? I mean, sure, it was a long time ago now, but hey, who knows, maybe we could end up finding them, right?" I tried to sound as enthusiastic, as optimistic, as humanly possible when I said this. I guess it was only fitting then when he told me what he did next.

"I DO know. They ain't missin'. Not no more..." I frowned.

"What do you mean? I thought you said--"

"I said I lost someone, not that they're missin'." I shrank back again.

"Oh..."

He sighed and, in a shaking voice, said, "She wasn't even in one piece when she was found. An arm here, one there, a leg over yonder, and her head..." He dropped his head into his hands and sobbed, "Oh Jesus..."

My heart stopped. This was the first time I'd heard of somebody actually being found in the mountains. Usually, you know, the stories all end with the person never being seen from again, but now...

"It was only a coupla months after she went missing, My little Darcy, she was, she was found all over the fuckin' mountain, in at least six different places, each with about five or six pieces of her."

"A-A couple of months?" I asked, my throat having gone dry now. He nodded his head.

And this little girl I'm after hasn't been gone for long...

Images of the girl I was searching for, being diced and quartered like she was a goddamn pork chop (pun intended -- I guess...), flooded my brain. This was quickly followed by the same images, only instead of the little girl, instead of any of the missing kids I'd seen from the posters, it was Bonnie.

"Save me, Roy!" I could hear her sweet little voice cry out to me. "They're hurting me! Roy! Daddy! Please, make them stop!" Then, it became a cacophony of all their voices, all crying out the same thing -- for me to save them.

But how can I when I don't know where they are?

"I-I'm... I'm... I'm sorry, I..."

"It's fine, just..." He sighed. "Look, I can appreciate what you're tryin' to do. It's a brave thing, really, but damn stupid as well. You're young, okay, an' unlike these poor youngin's here, you're not likely to end up in pieces for someone to find, not yet anyway."

"That's no reason for me to--"

"The hell it ain't, boy. Please, I'm beggin' you, just think about it for a minute 'fore you go doin' somethin' foolish. Please." I nodded before turning and walking out of the store in a daze. As blank as my head was, the walk from the door of the convenience store to the truck felt like I was walking on a damn treadmill; going forward but not actually going anywhere.

When I did make it back to the truck, about half an eternity later, the first thing out of Stacy's mouth was, "Um... Something wrong?" I remember looking at her, not actually seeing her really, but more like seeing behind her, if that makes any sense. Basically, I might as well have had the same sort of haunted, sort of "spaced out" look on my face that the cashier in the convenience store had a minute ago.

"Hello..." she said, waving her hand in my face. "Earth to Roy. Come in, Roy."

"Huh?"

"Oh, he's back."

"Huh? Oh uh... yeah."

"You okay?"

"Y-Yeah." I looked at my bag of chips and drink before realizing why I'd actually come here in the first place. "I'm uh, gonna go pump the gas."

"O-Okay..." She leaned back in her seat while I got out of the car. I was unhooking the pump when I noticed a faint sound in the distance. I looked out into the trees for a second. Nothing was out there and the sound didn't repeat again, so I went back to pumping the gas. My mind began stirring again, thinking about the children again, when it happened again. Because of how far afield my mind was at the time, though, I didn't actually realize it at first. It was the same thing that happens whenever you're asleep and your alarm clock goes off, but instead of waking you up, it travels into your dream and you just keep snoring right along.

It was that, only of course this not only wasn't even a dream -- more like a literal waking nightmare -- but I was awake (physically at least). Well, I didn't realize any sound had been made at all until it rang out again, a lot closer this time. My head snapped in the direction of the noise that I was almost sure for a second that I'd actually broken it, only to again see nothing. This time, I wasn't about to just brush it off.

I went to the passenger side window and knocked, rousing Stacy. She rolled down her window and asked what was up. "You hear that?" I asked.

"Hear what?"

"You didn't hear that noise?"

"What noise? Only noise I heard was you knocking on the window just now."

"You didn't hear that loud screeching just now?" She shook her head and opened her mouth to probably ask me if I was popping a screw loose upstairs when I heard it again. This time it was damn near deafening, like it was from something big, and right on top of me. Still, I couldn't see anything, but even still, there was no goddamn way she couldn't have heard it that time, or so I would've thought.

"Roy, what's going on?" she asked. I put my finger to my lips for a second. It didn't sound again, but I knew it was there -- whatever the hell IT was, of course.

"Listen." I whispered to her, "Didn't you hear that?"

"No, Roy, I don't hear a damn thing, now can we please go? If you're trying to fuck around with me here, it ain't funny." I looked at her, doing my best to convey with my face that I wasn't punking her here. I heard something. I don't know what, but I heard it, damn it. I remained prone for another two minutes before I heard the gas pump click, signaling I'd reached the $40 mark.

I quickly jammed the pump back into its place before scrambling back to the driver side of my truck. Right as I was about to open the door, I caught a glimpse of something deep in the trees on the other side of the road. It looked like two little flashlights, maybe even a couple of LEDs, paired evenly side by side with each other. I squinted to try and get a clearer look.

I couldn't see a damn thing. Everything was too damn dark. I could only barely make out the dark outlines of the trees. I did notice though that the lights appeared higher than they should be, meeting me at about eye level. Not only that, but I noticed they weren't so much shining as they were reflecting. I realized then these might not be lights at all...

But then, what the hell were they?

I leaned forward, still squinting. Still, I couldn't see a damn thing. I was actually about to start walking towards it (don't even ask me why, to this day, I still never understood why), but just as I was about to land the first step, Stacy pipes up going, "Roy, seriously, what the hell is going on with you? What're you lookin' at?" The lights, or refractions, whatever they were, suddenly went out. Then everything was shrouded in complete blackness again.

For another second, I kept looking at the woods, expecting to see them again, but nothing happened. I came slowly back to my senses and got back in the car. "So, you plan on telling me what the hell that was out there?" Stacy asked. I said nothing, not even regarding her as I drove off hurriedly. The next ten or twenty miles of the trip were ridden in silence. The whole time, all new images assaulted my brain.

Now, instead of just the kids crying out to me to save them, I was also imagining every type of beast or maniac that could've been standing there in the woods, apparently stalking me. I'd have probably kept driving the whole rest of the way like this, had it not been for the fact that only a few miles down from the gas station, there was someone standing in the middle of the road. I almost didn't see them, not until I had almost flattened them completely. I ended up slamming the brakes, giving both Stacy and I whiplash. "What the fuck?" I asked. I leaned forward, squinting my eyes.

"Who the hell is that?" Stacy asked, leaning forward to look as well. The person stood perfectly still. I pressed the horn twice. Neither time yielded any reaction. They were a perfect statue in front of us. What the hell? Why's this dude just standing there?

I tried inching the truck forward. I spent the better part of two minutes doing this; just trying to scare this person into moving out of the way, but he wouldn't. I came right on top of him and laid on the horn. Nothing.

"Is this guy deaf and blind?" I asked.

"Roy... I don't think that's a guy." I looked at her, cocking my eyebrows.

"What do you mean?"

"He's too short to be a guy. I think that's a kid out there." My eyes grew. Looking closer, I realized she was right. Whoever the hell this was couldn't have been an inch over 4.5 ft tall.

"Okay, but still, why isn't he moving?" Stacy opened her mouth but didn't say anything, simply shaking her head while shrugging. I looked back to the road ahead. The kid still stood there, motionless, lifeless, looking more like a scarecrow than an actual kid.

I blared at him one last time before opening the door.

"Whoa, what're you doing?" asked Stacy.

"Stay here, I'm gonna see what's going on here." I got out and shut the door, hearing Stacy tell me to be careful. I started walking over to the kid. "Hey there." I called out to him. He didn't move. "Hey uh... You lost, buddy?" Nothing.

Maybe he's deaf, blind, AND dumb? I finally reached him and went to tap on his face when I froze dead in my tracks. I don't know how I didn't see it before, but this kid's face wasn't his actual face at all. It was a sort of paper plate cutout mask, like what kids make in kindergarten for Art class. It wasn't a regular paper plate either, it looked like one of those ZooPal plates, but with the eye and nose holes cut out of it.

I went to take off the mask and as soon as the tip of my index finger came in contact with it, I heard glass shattering, followed by a mix of sounds; both of Stacy screaming and of high pitched squealing. My head jerked back just long enough to see about five or maybe even six small figures climbing all over the truck. Before I could do anything though, I felt something latch onto me from behind.

2

I didn't have any chance to look, react, or even form half a coherent thought before sharp pain shot through my body from my ear lobe. The kid's arms quickly wrapped around my face and he began using his fingers to try and gouge out my eyes. Stacy's screams increased in pitch, as did the squeals from the others on the truck.

"Stacy!" I shouted. I found this to be a mistake though when the kid's fingers decided then to go from my eyes to trying to pry my fuckin' jaws apart. When this proved to be unsuccessful, I guess, the kid then switched from that to trying to just force his hands down my throat to choke me out. I tried as hard as I could to shake the little fucker off of me, but whatever sort of exercises or whatever this kid had been doing, it was effective because I couldn't make him let go, no matter what.

Finally, I had to resort to biting down while he had his hands down inside my mouth. This thankfully worked and he let go. He fell off of me, squealing like the others were. Now freed, I made a break back for the truck to rescue Stacy. By that time, the others, all of them kids with the same paper plate pig masks by the way, were swarming her, climbing all over her, biting her, jerking her hair out.

One of them, I managed to see, ripped away a handful that also took a decent chunk of her scalp with it.

Some of them had sticks, too, which they were using to bludgeon her across the face. I made it back to the truck, only to have two of them spring from the passenger side window at me. Both of them were the stick wielding ones too, and so I ended up taking two strikes across my face, knocking me flat on my back on the asphalt. My head instantly went dizzy and it only got worse when they then decided knocking me down wasn't enough and proceeded to stove my face into the dirt until I lost consciousness completely. The last thing I'd just faintly see and hear were the sounds of Stacy's screams.

They carried into my sleep, too; the screams. The squealing, too, all of it. I could see all of the kids in my dreams, surrounding me.

***

They stare at me. I can't see their eyes, but I can feel their gazes, hateful and ravenous, beating down on my head like UV rays from the sun. They all squeal and shriek maniacally, raring up to charge at me and to rip me apart, devouring me. Their faces change rapidly between those of kids to those of the pig masks.

They have no pupils in their eyes. They're all coal black and lifeless, inhuman. I get a closer look at their faces, their "normal" faces and I find that they all look familiar. I can't explain it because of everything that's happening, but I know I've seen the faces before. They charge at me and pounce.

They swarm me, just like they swarmed Stacy, and in less than seconds, my arms and legs are restrained to the ground. I fight rigorously to break free, but it's no use. Their grips, despite being just small children, are iron vices on my wrists and ankles. I scream in agony, which is easily drowned under their chaotic squealing. Their eyes collectively beat down on me, each empty of any emotion or feeling except hunger.

Suddenly they all part ways, save for the ones holding me down. A bellowing squeal rumbles through the ground beneath me. My heart stops, my body seizes. In front of me, I watch a gargantuan figure take shape, lording over me. Its breath is hot, like his nostrils are geysers, billowing blistering steam right down into my face.

It's cloaked completely in darkness, completely cloaking any of its features. From its outline, though, I can briefly see two small shapes protruding from the top of the beast's head. Small, lopsided, triangular shaped protrusions I take to be its ears. This, mixed with the appearance of its lumpy head and what looks to me to be a snout, leads me to realize this thing, this beast looming over me, about to devour me, is none other than the legend itself; "Pig Man".

Another deafening, earth shaking squeal is blasted right down into my face. I feel the blood inside me freeze solid in each and every limb. The others around me join in, creating a primal dissonance that lingers in the air even long after they cease. The beast raises what looks to me like an ax in the air. With a single, powerful downward swing, the head of the ax comes down and...

***

I woke up then, shooting into an upright position. Everything around me was dark and I felt a searing pain in my lower half. Imagine you were shitting shards of jagged fiberglass, now imagine that, but instead of it coming out of your butt, it's coming from your legs. That's exactly what it felt like when I woke up.

I attempted to move, only to find that, aside from of course the excruciating pain amplifying when I did, I was also restricted by some sort of rope or something around my wrist. It took almost a full minute to realize something was majorly off about me. Where my legs were, I realized they felt a lot lighter than they should've been. I tried wiggling my toes or something, figuring maybe my feet were asleep or something somehow, only to find that that wasn't it.

My feet weren't numb, they weren't there at all!

I went to try and grab at my legs, but couldn't move far enough thanks to the rope. I raised my right leg up as far as I could, bearing through the pain that came with this action as much as I could, to find my fears confirmed. In just the pale glimmer of soft moonlight that a small crack in the walls or ceiling I was in, I found that my foot was gone, severed just below the calf. It wasn't bleeding, indicating to me they must've cauterized it or something, but it was, it was gone.

I looked close to find the same was true for the other foot as well. BOTH of my feet were fucking gone! My heart went from zero to a thousand in less than a second. My head swung everywhere, not at all knowing what or where I was looking for.

Where the hell am I? What the fuck happened, who cut off my fucking feet? Why? Why am I here? Where's--

Then my heart stopped completely. Up to that point, my mind was a blur, nothing but a blank cloud, swimming around in my skull. Then I remembered Stacy and everything else started to come running back to me all at once. I looked up to where the small ounce of moonlight was bleeding in from.

Stacy! Oh God, where is she?! Is she alright? Is she even still...

I shook my head. No, get your shit together. You panic now and you're finished for sure. You don't know that Stacy's gone yet, so for now, we just assume she's alive. For right now, just find a way out of here.

I caught a deep, cleansing breath. Sure enough, the little birdie in my head actually managed to help me, allowing me to relax, even if only a little bit. In situations like this, you know, a little bit of relief helps a lot. So the first thing I did was reassess to myself the situation. I was in a darkened room or box of some sort, chained to a bed by my wrists, and my feet have been amputated (something I still wonder, by the way, how I didn't notice until I woke up).

I squinted at the hole. That must be the opening for what or wherever this is. So, okay, just gotta go out through there...

Of course, how in the hell was I supposed to do that with no legs and no arms? So, being that sneaking out was ruled out as an option, I started thinking again about the situation itself. The fact that I was tied up, despite having removed my feet already, denoted to me whoever had brought me here planned on coming back for me at some point. That, and the fact that they'd left the crack in the ceiling. They didn't want me to go anywhere, but it wasn't likely they were wanting me to die yet, either. Think about it, if they'd wanted me dead, why bother cauterizing my wounds after amputating instead of letting me bleed out?

In other words, they still needed me. For what was anybody's guess, but the fact remained, and therefore it was likely whoever it was would be coming back for me at some point. The challenge then was to be able to last long enough without passing out or dying of thirst, hunger, or any number of other things that were likely to kill me until that happened. Thankfully, "smart" as my old man thought I was, I did indeed have some of his foolishness in me, enough to embolden me to begin howling and shouting obscenities at the top of my lungs to alert them that I was awake and hopefully come to me. Then I'd have a possible opportunity.

Obviously, it was improv as to what I'd do if and when they did come. Like I said, there was no way of telling why they were keeping me alive this long, and therefore there was also no way to know what they'd do in response to me showing them my ass either. In instances like this though, you take whatever opportunities you can afford and make the best of the rest as you go along. I ended up shrieking my head off for the next ten or twelve minutes, until my throat felt like it'd just been made to swallow shards of glass. Oddly, it wasn't until about 3 or 4 minutes after the noise died down that I thought I heard someone stomping toward me.

There were multiple footfalls, each of them having to scurry along like mice. The kids, I thought. I braced myself for whatever I figured was coming to me once they reached me. The footfalls reached the door, but nothing happened. I held my breath, expecting the door to fly right open and the kids to pour in and swarm me, but they didn't. I opened my eyes and saw the door was still closed.

The hell are they waiting for? I opened my mouth to try shrieking again, but nothing would come out. My voice was far too gone by that point. I heard something slide to the right from the door, like a bolt or something, before the door slowly creaked open. When it was just opened enough, something big was flung onto the floor. After that, I watched two of them trot into the room and start dragging it closer to the bed.

I looked to see what it was, only to immediately wish I hadn't. It was someone's decapitated body. The head, right arm, and left leg were gone. The kids dragged it over the rest of the way to the bed. Before I could struggle or do anything, two of them came onto the bed and began grabbing me, forcing me still and prying my mouth open forcefully. Then, squealing like crazy, the last one took out what looked to me like a meat cleaver he'd had stashed in the back of his pants.

He started haphazardly hacking away at the remaining arm before taking the severed limb and force-feeding it to me. I did my absolute damnedest to struggle, but shamefully, for whatever reason, it was like I was trying to struggle against two full grown muscle men. I know they were just kids, but seriously, they were strong! The kid shoves the arm in my mouth and forces it to go down my throat. I immediately start choking.

The room filled with their squeals while this was happening, drowning my groans and gasps for mercy. The two holding my mouth open even began moving my jaws up and down to make me actually chew the fucking thing. All of it was thick and chewy, so much so that swallowing any of it almost caused me to suffocate. Finally, the one with the cleaver let out a howling squeal that silenced the others. The two holding me let go then and stepped down from the bed to join the others.

They dragged the body away back through the door, shutting and bolting it back. I was left sitting up on my bed, mouth stuffed with raw flesh, feeling weak and overall violated. What had just happened; I mean, besides the whole being force-fed human flesh thing? Was this just their way of shutting me up? They decided to gag me like that just to keep me quiet, maybe?

But then... Why wouldn't they have just killed me?

I thought then about how I couldn't have moved or done anything if I tried -- which God knows I did. If the purpose was to silence me, then why did they want to leave me alive? Why wouldn't they want me to make noise? Sure, I could see it being irritating as hell to have to listen to that constantly, something I'm sure those little bastards had experience with, but even still, the question remains, what difference did it make to silence me?

But then, what if maybe it wasn't about silencing me at all? What if they were already going to come, what if they were going to do that, regardless of whether or not I made noise? So okay, they wanted to keep me alive... But why feed me, unless...

Unless the idea was to fatten me up.

I thought about the brief glimpse of the body they dragged in. The person, whoever they once were, was a pudgy one. Not overweight, perhaps, but big enough that they could butcher them and their parts would make quite a few mouthfuls. You know... Just like a pig...

I had to get out then. I knew what my purpose to them was, and now I had to escape if I wanted to get out with my life and, at least hopefully, Stacy's as well. I looked around again. There still wasn't any sort of tool or anything I could use to get myself free. Or was there?

See, I didn't notice it until a minute or so later, but the little twerp from earlier had apparently gotten clumsy and left his cleaver behind. If I could reach the cleaver, there was a chance I could cut the ropes tying my wrists to the bed. It didn't look all that big, granted, but I mean, it cut through flesh easily enough apparently, so I figured it shouldn't have much, if any trouble at all with plain old, probably worn rope, right? Tricky part came though in trying to actually reach the damn thing with both hands tied. I laid just a foot or two away from the bed, so I leaned forward, bearing all of my weight at once on the edge of the bed.

It was surprisingly (well, sort of) tough to make the bed tip over, but eventually it did, where the objective then was to grab the cleaver and cut the ropes. Fortunately, this actually proved to be not quite as difficult to pull off, despite having very limited reach. I seized the cleaver and began a combination of hacking and sawing at the ropes. Even more to my luck, I turned out to be right about the ropes being worn because after only about ten, maybe fifteen whacks, the fucker snapped loose, freeing my right arm. The other one admittedly took a little bit longer, about 25 to 30 whacks, but all the same, it snapped too.

Once both arms were free, I began the real ordeal; having to slug my way out of the room and somehow maneuver, without getting caught by the kids or anything/one else skulking around, throughout what or wherever the hell this place was. My arms already felt like wet, boiled pasta, and my leg -- the good leg -- felt weak as well. Still, I knew that staying wasn't an option, unless I develop a fancy for both eating human flesh and being eaten myself. Whatever it took, I had to get the fuck out of there.

I made it out of the room somewhat easily enough, at least given the circumstances, but when I got out into the hallway, I found out just how much more I'd bitten off than what I could chew. The long, hardly lit hallway stretched for almost a mile, or at least a good fifteen to twenty feet, and the floor itself was slick, giving me nothing to even grab or dig my nails into to be able to try and pull myself along. The good news was, at the end of this hall, the door was wide open. I wouldn't have to open it or anything, just get through it.

I pulled along as hard as I could, doing my best not to make any noise, lest I attract the kids again. At one point, about maybe a quarter or perhaps half of the way through, I froze. On the floor above me, elephantine footsteps rushed across, each one simultaneously rocking the entire hallway as well as causing my heart to cut cartwheels in my chest. They boomed all throughout the hall, too, sounding like gunshots with each step. Somehow I didn't end up going deaf because of this, though that might not exactly be a great thing because I guarantee you that what I heard accompanying all of this was nothing short of sickening.

The best way I know how to describe the sounds I heard above me is that it sounded like a very large dog was growling while congested, muffling it somewhat, while its mouth was full and chewing at the same time. The footsteps stopped at about the middle of the ceiling and for a moment, everything around me was completely still. I was about to start slugging forward again when my body instantly just locked up at the blasting of the most inhuman sort of roar I'd ever heard. It sounded like the squealing of a thousand pigs while they were on steroids, somehow coming together to form one body and emanate from one throat.

I still feel sick to my fucking stomach when I think about that. Hell, I wanted to throw up right then and there in the hallway, coupling both that sound, the grumbling sort of sounds from before, and the god awful miasma that'd been choking me ever since the second I woke up chained to the bed. I couldn't though. My stomach, like the rest of me, was frozen solid on the floor. I then heard two or three stomps in place where they were standing, followed by another squealing roar. That time, I'm almost sure my heart actually stopped.

Another moment of silent stillness passed before then being followed by another series of stomps in the forward direction. Eventually, the stomps faded away, but even still, it was at least another 20 to 25 whole minutes before my body shook itself out of entropy and got moving again. Once I was, I found myself using every ounce of strength imaginable, using the imagery I had of whatever the unholy hell THAT was as motivation to keep pushing, ignoring how tired I was in reality.

My arms were screaming at me. I thought I was going to end up working them so hard to move along that they were going to end up just popping right off the sockets of my shoulders. I kept pulling though. I had to get out. I had to find Stacy. I had to find the kid. I have to save them. I have to...

I have to save...

Oh god...

***

"Roy! Help me!"

Stacy! Hang on, I'm coming!

"They're hurting me, Roy!"

"Save us!"

Just hang in there, everybody, I'm coming! I'm gonna get you all outta here!

"Why weren't you there, Roy?"

No... No, not now...

"You can't save anybody, not even your baby sis."

B-Bonnie...

"Noone's ever gonna find them. Or you. You can't save anybody!"

***

"NO!"

My breath caught in my throat almost immediately after the last echo left my throat. Sure enough, in my little breakdown there, I'd managed to make it the rest of the way to the open doorway. Ahead of me was a room that appeared to be, from what I could actually see of it anyways, like some sort of gross looking meat locker, with large hunks of pork (well, what I would think was cuts of pork, had I not already known any better) hanging from chains to the ceiling.

I pushed myself further, not wasting any time to try and survey the area or anything. As I came to find out in just a couple seconds, this was not my best choice. From the other end of the room, the elephantine stomping came back, this time, heading straight for where I was. Out of sheer luck and absolutely nothing else, I managed to hurl myself like a spear into a hidden corner of the room just before the door swung open. From the crevice I wormed my way into, I watched two large hooves stomp into the room. Yes, hooves, not feet.

The disgusting grumbling or congested growling noise returned too. I did see as well a pair of legs, squirming and kicking. Whoever this was was still alive.

Oh Christ, this person's about to be butchered!

Part of me felt the overwhelming urge to go out there and do... well, I don't know, but something other than laying there, watching. I swallowed this down, though, knowing good and damn well I couldn't do anything to whatever this behemoth was if I tried. I watched the pair of panicking legs raise higher in the air and accompanying this was a woman's panicked shrieking. Alarms sounded in my head and it was everything I could do to stay put.

Oh Jesus GOD, please, not Stacy. Not her.

I heard the thing squeal furiously at its victim, causing her to shriek louder. In another instant, her shrieks became ear-splitting, anguished. I closed my eyes and covered my ears but it did me no good. Her screaming still bled through, becoming a catalyst for a lifetime of night terrors to come. The monster stomped away then, leaving the legs dangling there while their owner tore her lungs to shreds.

I stayed in my hiding spot, utterly speechless, no clue whatsoever as to what in the unholy hell I was supposed to do. I mean, what would YOU have done in this situation? "I'd try to save her", yeah right. What the fuck would you be able to do with ONE LEG, NO STRENGTH IN YOUR ARMS OR LEGS, and not even any basic first aid supplies to help a woman who basically just got turned into a goddamn windchime?

Look, I'm sorry if that sounds aggressive, but that really was the dilemma I was faced with right then. I wanted to help, obviously -- it was the entire reason I came up this godforsaken mountain in the first fuckin' place -- but I couldn't! I couldn't save the woman. I couldn't protect Stacy.

("Why Roy? Why weren't you there for me, big brother?")

I can't save any of the kids. I can't save the girl. I can't...

("You'll never get out of here. No one will ever find you.")

I can't save...

("This is all your fault, Roy. You can't protect anybody, not even your own baby sis.")

I'm... I'm sorry. I'm sorry Stacy. I'm sorry everybody...

And God, Bonnie, I'm so sorry I can't be there for you.

I was shook from another breakdown by the sound of little feet pounding toward the room from the door I'd come through. It was the kids, likely looking for me, or so I thought. They must've come through to torture me again and found that I'd flown the coop. This was more than enough to light a bonfire under my ass and get myself moving with as much speed as my arms could manage pulling me along. I slithered my way out of the little crevice and began slugging forward, doing my best not to look at the hanging body (which was still twitching and moaning in agony, by the way). I'd just about made it to the door when I heard the door behind me get swung open.

I froze then. There was nowhere to throw myself into this time, and I'd already crawled too far away from the one I was in before to try that again. No, I was screwed this time. I couldn't run, couldn't fight, and couldn't even hide. I closed my eyes. This was it, yet again.

The kids all poured into the room, all squealing madly, and my body seized up, preparing for them to snatch me up and drag me away. Hell, honestly, part of me thought they'd 86 the whole dragging me back to the room part and just do me right there in the meat locker. I opened my eyes though when I realized that nothing was happening. I was still alive, untouched. When I looked behind me, I watched the kids jerking down the woman's body from the large ass meat hook she was skewered on, flaying open her back completely, before then just diving right in like she was a birthday cake at a party.

Without manners, dignity, or remorse, those kids just devoured her handful after handful. This time, I couldn't help it, I threw up. And just my luck, too, the little bastards heard me and immediately lost interest in their present victim. I tried scurrying across the floor out the door but it was far too late. They snatched me up by my stump of a left leg and immediately dragged me back into the meat locker. Using my other leg, I tried kicking them off me as best I could but that was no use either. They were like a horde of ants; each one I kicked off, about two more jumped in their place.

They had me smothered and at least two or three of them had sticks, too, which you best believe they put to good use on me. I'm not sure, but I want to say the fuckers managed to at least crack, if not break entirely, five of my ribs as well as a few other bones before knocking me out with a hammer strike across my face. That time I was sure that was it. I was dead.

To my chagrin, this wasn't the case and what I'd wake up to next is something that'd make any person immediately wish for death. I was woken by the most searing pain I'd ever felt shooting down my left leg. I found myself suspended a full two feet off the ground by my left foot, my good one. When I looked up, I was immediately both sickened and horrified to see that a hook was now skewered straight through it. A small river of blood slowly traveled down from the burning, aching gash. I was horrified, yet in too much pain to scream, in shock or in pain.

Imagine that for a second, that you can't even make a sound or react in any way physically because of how severe the pain is. You're in the worst form of Hell at that point, unable to react to the pain or make it end, yet not severe enough still to kill you, at least not immediately. The only way I knew the pain would end now is to wait for me to pass out or straight up pass away from suspension. The silver lining of this was that, either from the aforementioned process itself or from blood loss, this didn't take long to take effect.

In seconds, the world went blurry and my arms, the only limbs I was still able to use, went numb. Even still, it was like something in me still fought to stay awake. Ironic, isn't it? The one time you find yourself wishing you could just slip away, and survival instinct itself betrays you. So there I was, hanging from the ceiling, disoriented, weak, and basically half dead. At that point, any ambition I had to play the hero had been long obliterated. At that point, I'd have honestly been happy if I could've made it out of there at all OUTSIDE of a body bag, with or without Stacy or any of the kids.

It was faint, but I could hear a sound from somewhere in the room around me, soft and faint. I realized that it was the sound of someone crying. Because of my blurry ass vision, plus the lack of lighting in the room itself, I couldn't see who or where it was coming from, but I could still tell it was there, somewhere at my right. I could tell it was another young woman, too.

"S-St-St-Sta-Sta-cy?" The girl kept crying, sniffling. "Sta-cy... is... that... you?"

The crying stopped, devolving into sniffles. "Who-Who's there?" The voice was small and pathetic sounding, but clear enough for me to realize that it wasn't Stacy's voice. I didn't know what to do or say now. I heard movement coming from the corner where I heard the girl's voice. From the shadowed corner, I watched a young girl crawl out and my heart damn near stopped completely for a third time that day. It was the girl from the poster, THE girl I'd come all this fucking way , enduring all of this torture for.

She was right there, crouched in a corner. She was alive. I'd found her...

I haven't failed...

I found her...

She crawled out until she was about a half a foot away from my face before stopping. "A-A-Am-Ame-lia..." Her eyes grew a bit. "Ame-lia... H-Hill..."

"Who are you? H-How do you know my name?" I wanted to tell her everything. I wanted to tell her that I'd come to rescue her and her father. I wanted to tell her that my cousin was missing and that I had to rescue her as well. I wanted to tell her just how much it meant to me that I could actually see her right then. Even if I couldn't do anything else, just seeing her actually meant something; that this whole crusade from Hell wasn't in vain.

My mouth opened, but instead of any of the thoughts I just mentioned, all that came out was "P-Pos-ter."

"What?" she asked. I raised my arms as best I could, which is to say not much at all.

"Pos-ter... In p-pock-et..." She slowly rose up until she was on her feet. Her hand cautiously, shakily reached out to my right side pocket and dug around, pulling out the folded up "Missing Persons' ' poster. She unfolded it and skimmed over it for about three seconds before dropping both it and her jaw.

"Y-You came... for me?" she asked. I said nothing. She scoffed in amazement. Her face said it all, the classic look of disbelief. I couldn't necessarily blame her, but it broke my heart all the same. Then it straight up shattered when she broke down into tears while seizing me into her tightest bearhug.

"Oh my God! You're here! You're here! God listened!" I was confused. Who was she talking about? I couldn't bring myself to ask, but it didn't matter anyway because what she said next actually made my eyes overflow with tears. "You're an angel, aren't you? I asked God to send an angel and you came!"

I couldn't tell what hurt worse, honestly. The fact that this sweet little girl had been so desensitized, so mentally jacked, that she would look at me, an ordinary guy who just wanted to do something good, and genuinely believe that I'm a divine savior, or the fact that, in spite of coming all this way, in spite of her being right there, I still couldn't be that for her.

"H-Help... Me..." She paused, staring blankly at me. "H-Help... Me... Down..." Her eyes darted up and down from my foot to my face. "P-Ple-ase..."

She began shaking again as she rose up and reached for my foot. I clamped my eyes shut, doing everything I could to steel myself for the absolute WORLD of agony that was about to come rushing my way in a moment. I could feel her slender, tender fingers brush the top of my foot, hesitant to actually try doing anything. "I... I... I can't..."

"Please... H-Hel-p m-me down..." Adrenaline was wearing off now, taking my consciousness with it. I knew it was a damn good bet that if I clocked out now, still skewered from the ceiling, there wasn't a good chance at all that I'd be waking back up again. I couldn't let that happen, not after making it this far. I needed her help now just as much as she needed mine.

I felt her begin to push up on my foot to unhook it and not even two seconds in, I was having to hold my breath to keep from screaming bloody fuckin' murder. What was worse was that she wasn't all that strong, never even mind the fact that she's probably not eaten much in the past three months she'd been missing, so she struggled like hell trying to even lift up my foot enough. At one point, her grip slipped and the hook sunk further into my foot than before. That was when I did cry out in pain.

"I'm sorry!" she cried. "God, I-I can't do it!" She started backing away. "I can't do it, I'm not--"

"It's fine!" I said through gritted teeth. My foot was on fire still, but I knew I had to suck it up through the pain if I was gonna be able to have her help me. She stepped forward and started again. It was a lot more painful this time, her trying to get the hook out of my foot. When it slipped last time, it must've severed a good few more tendons, and so her trying to pull it out again felt like she was trying to pull the bones in my foot out of the skin.

Through all of this, though, both she and I endured. "Hang on... Almost got it..." Suddenly a huge release of pressure was relieved from my foot and I fell limply to the floor. I was free. I'd found Amelia, and I was free again. But what now?

"What are we gonna do?" she asked me.

"I... I... I don't..." I grew drowsy. It wasn't just a physical exhaustion, either. It was like I was a computer, with both the internal and external hard drives both overheating and shutting everything down. After everything up to that point, I needed to "Clock out" so to speak. Of course, I knew I couldn't do that, not yet, not if I wanted myself and this little girl to perhaps have a chance at making it off this mountain alive. Somehow, I managed to continue fighting the urge to fade out but doing so essentially exhausted all of my physical strength (what little of it remained anyway) and most of my mental stamina as well.

She apparently saw this too and went to look for something, I couldn't tell what at first. She walked over toward the back of the room and came back with this large bowl of water. "Here, drink up."

She turned me over onto my back and cradled my head to drink from the bowl. My mouth fell open and I drank like a damn pack mule. Fortunately, the water had enough in it to wake me up at least, even if I still couldn't actually do much. She took the bowl away and I rose slowly to a sitting position and surveyed the room.

The room itself was at least average sized. Spacious, but not enough to fit too too much inside. More like a secondary freezer, probably just right next to the one the kids jumped me in earlier. This also made sense because of the appearance of a bunch of containers filled with what I could only assume was any number of organs or guts from past victims. I figured, given that this place here acted much like a regular slaughterhouse, that they kept one room for the actual meat and hides themselves, while keeping the smaller entrails, vegetables and shit in another room.

To me, this meant one of two things. The first is that the door to this particular room at the far end ahead of me would lead to a dead end, maybe just another spare cooler room or something. The second possibility is that it led towards some place like a den or a dining room or just some sort of personal room or office maybe. I figured this because, looking at Amy, I couldn't help but wonder why she hadn't thought of trying to actually go out through there.

"What's behind this door?" I asked, pointing to the door ahead of us. She shrank down.

"That's where they're keeping us." she replied with a continuously shrinking voice. I could hear her throat cracking as she spoke. "I... I managed to get myself out of there, but then I had to hide in here when they brought you in and..." Her eyes diverted down to my foot. My eyes remained on the door.

So there ARE still others. And if they're in this room, then that means...

I began scooting myself toward the door. "What are you doing?" she asked. I made it to the door and reached up for the knob but I was too short to reach from my position. "What're you doing, we can't go back in there!"

"We have to get them out, too, don't we?" She shrank back down again at this. "Here, help me with the door, I can't reach high enough." She stood still, quivering violently.

"N-No, w-we can't."

"What do you mean, why can't we? We have to."

"You don't understand, they're all... They're all..." She started nodding forward like she was retching.

"They're all what?" She said nothing, just continued to stand there. "They're all what, Amy?"

"They're... They're all... changed!" I frowned.

"What're you talking about, changed how?"

"I... I don't know. but they're all different. They aren't kids anymore. I watched a lot of the ones that were taken here after me start to go crazy. They started killing each other if one of them didn't act like they did. That's why I had to get out of there, before they came for me next."

My hand froze and my eyes grew. I was wrong with both assumptions. It was neither a fridge room or a den, it was a pig pen. Not only that, but her words right then confirmed my suspicions, that these little maniacs were the same kids from the posters. My stomach began turning over as I opened my mouth and choked out, "W-Why?"

"I-I don't know, okay? I just don't. They just started going crazy, squealing and everything, just like the big one, and started eating those of us that wouldn't lose their minds. Then, the big one would come back and let them out to hunt for more on the mountain like you and me."

I paused, drinking all of this in, choking on it as it went down. The legends were true. All of them. "Pig Man" was real, and he had every trait the legends spoke of; a gargantuan beast with the ability to muddle a person's mind, as well as snap them in half like a twig and devour them whole. It was all real, and now I had proof. Now, I also knew what was really happening to everyone that disappeared. In that vein, I couldn't tell whose fate was worse; those who were butchered in horrific ways, with the last thing they'd see being their friend, brother, daughter, what have you, savagely devouring them without a care in the world, or the actual freaks themselves, who God himself only knows what kind of psychological torture they underwent to push them towards cannibalizing their loved ones like that.

It's like when you look at zombies, right? It's easy to think that the victims have it the worst, until you stop to think about what the zombies themselves have to endure, wondering if even a remote part of who they used to be still lingers somewhere, deep down, and if that part of them is appalled at what they have to do now. I say this because the next question I asked her puts this into perspective a little bit. "How... How did you get out?"

She didn't reply to this. I could see that she couldn't have said anything if she wanted to. I didn't need her to, though. The way I watched her face, her dirty, exhausted, yet still sweet and innocent looking face, just up and melt told me exactly everything I needed to know. She raised her palms up, showing off dirty, clotted bloodstains. She began to sob and I outstretched my arms. "Come here... Come here, it's okay." She threw herself into my arms, burying her face in my chest.

I held her close and whispered, "Shh... It's okay. It's gonna be okay, I promise." From my chest, I could hear her crying, "I didn't want to! I didn't want to" over and over again. My hands ran through her frizzled hair that seemed faded now from its more vibrant appearance on the poster. I'd have held her forever -- she needed it, and it wasn't like anyone else was around to do it anymore anyway. I was forced to let her go, however, when we heard small footsteps approaching again. She scurried back into her little hidey hole she came out of while I sprawled out my arms and legs, doing my best to appear dead, hoping to fucking GOD these little fuckers wouldn't either go poking or prodding to make sure or anything like that or worse, try to restring my ass back to the ceiling.

3

I closed my eyes right as the door swung open. I heard them clamor in, immediately running for the hook, where I was. Shit, they're coming for me... Okay, just stay calm, don't make any sort of movements.

Try as I did not to, my body couldn't help but tense up, anticipating at any moment for one or two of them to start beating the hell out of me with their sticks again. I heard their feet moving around me, but nothing was happening. That is, until I felt hands grab up my arms and begin dragging me away. It took everything in me then not to freak out and blow my cover. Oh God, what're they doing with me? They're gonna string me back up again, aren't they? Oh God, please not again!

I felt them continue dragging me along. I squinted one of my eyes open to see that I was being dragged into the room I'd been trying to open earlier, the one Amelia had come from. They dropped my arms before scurrying back to the other room. I opened my eyes fully when I heard the door shut. Looking around, I found that the room I was in now was small, each wall lined with these sort of wooden boxes, similar to a chicken coop almost. Like every other room in this godforsaken place, this one was largely dark, with the only light coming from a single lightbulb dangling in the center of the room just a few inches above me.

My neck ached when I tried to arch it upwards. My breath was steady, despite being two seconds from wanting to panic. I wasn't sure if anyone was actually in the room with me or not, but regardless, I knew I couldn't afford to end up attracting the kids' attention again or worse, end up getting Pig Man himself coming after me. "Oh my God." cried a soft, broken voice from my right. I turned my head and damn near lost all the breath in my body. "Roy! Oh my God, are you okay?!"

"St-Stacy." She scurried out from one of the boxes along the wall.

"Oh God, Roy, are you--" Her words caught in her throat. She brought her hands up to her mouth and I knew it was everything she could do to not scream. Somehow -- to this day, I can't tell you how -- I managed to actually find it in me to chuckle.

"It's... It's not... Not as bad as it looks..."

"Oh sweet Jesus Christ on a stick, Roy, "Not as bad as it looks"? For fuck's sake, you look like a shredded carcass already." I held up my hands.

"I promise, I'm fine, okay?" Irony decided to be a real bitch right after I said that by sending a jolt of searing pain straight through my leg and throughout my body. I groaned.

"Uh huh, sure." She began trying to take up my arms to drag me out of there.

"Whoa, what the hell are you doing?"

"What does it look like? I'm getting us the hell out of this hellhole."

"Wait, do you even know where the hell to go?" She stopped and dropped my arms, sighing.

"Shit, you're right, no I don't." She turned away toward the wooden coops and shouted "FUCK!"

"Shh! Are you trying to get them to come back after us?" She sighed again.

"Well what're we supposed to do then?"

"I... I don't know yet, okay?" She scoffed.

"Oh, real helpful tip, Cous."

"Look, what the hell do you expect, okay? I've had to wing it this entire goddamn time."

"Oh yeah, and that looks like it's been working wonders for ya, stumpy."

"Fuck you, okay? I didn't even want to do this, okay?"

"The fuck do you mean, "You didn't wanna do this"? Last I checked, YOU were the one wanting to play Superman to save some little girl you'd never even fuckin' seen before."

"And last I checked, I told YOU that I was looking to 86 the whole operation, but NO..." A brief moment of silence passed, with tension forming a noose around both our throats. Finally I sighed and said, "Look, this isn't helping either of us. We need to focus on getting the three of us out of here and--"

"Whoa, wait a minute, check your counting there, Roy. What do you mean "Three"?"

"You, me, and Amelia." Her eyebrows cocked sideways at me.

"Amelia?" she asked. "Who's that?"

"The girl from the poster, remember?"

"Yeah, what about her?" It took her a moment, just like it took me a moment back at my Dad's house, to catch on to the implication. "Wait, you're telling me you actually found her?" I nodded. "Fuck, Roy, why didn't you tell me?"

"Because A, you hadn't given me the chance to say much, and B, because I honestly thought you'd already known, seeing as how she said she'd come out of here."

"Wait, she came out of here?"

"Yeah."

"Just like the rest of those little freaks?"

"Yeah."

"Roy... I don't think she's--"

"Don't even say it, okay? She's not one of them, I promise. Those kids couldn't feel like she could. She still has a sound, if probably scarred for eternity, mind." Stacy wasn't convinced. I sighed and said to her, "Look, I'll show you, just help me out of here and you'll see, okay?"

"And if she isn't "Sound of mind", what're you gonna do? You ain't exactly in fighting shape, you know."

"Look, we've come this far, okay? I'd feel better knowing we at least did what we came here to do." The two of us just stared at each other, deadlocked in an impasse. I'll admit, I couldn't necessarily blame her for thinking the way she was. She had an obvious point about one thing; I wasn't in any shape to fight (or even flight for that matter) my way out of any situation that might come up. Not to mention what Amelia herself told me about how she even got out in the first place.

She had no choice though. She HAD to to get away, right? This led my train of thought in another direction, though. What about the other kids, the ones that DID go feral, did they lose themselves willingly? Now on most days, I'd have answered no without hesitation. They were kids for Christ's sake, and captivated ones at that. Of course they wouldn't have done this to themselves and each other unless... Unless...

Unless they had to.

I was actually on the verge of conceding my point when she caved and said, pointing at the door, "Fine, let's get moving then. You said she was out there?" I nodded and she took up my arms. "Come on." She strained herself trying to tug me along. For a second, I couldn't help wondering just how the hell those kids were able to tow my ass around, yet my adult cousin, it's everything she can do to not collapse. Whatever Pig Man's got 'em on, it's some powerful shit.

She was able to heave me across the floor to the door before having to stop to catch her breath. She opened the door then and gasped. I arched my neck up to see that, after dragging me into this room, they'd strung another poor bastard up in my place. Whoever it was was male, young, around 16 or 17 maybe, and was missing his head while his arms and legs were hogtied behind his back with butcher's twine.

"What in the--"

"Stacy!" I called out, snapping her attention back to me. "Forget about that, come on." She passed a glance back and forth between me and the hallway ahead before taking up my arms again. She heaved me along until about the center of the hallway before she had to stop again.

"Fuck, Roy..." groaned Stacy. "I don't know that I can keep pulling you along like this." I said nothing to this. From my right again, I heard Amelia's small voice.

"You're okay!" I looked over to see her crawling out of her hiding spot from earlier. "Oh my God, I thought they were gonna..." She trailed off, looking at Stacy.

"I take it you're Amelia?" asked Stacy. Amelia nodded.

"How do you know my name? Did you see the poster, too?"

"You bet your ass I did, same as ol' stumpy here, and thanks to this genius, now we're both catching all different flavors of Hell." I snickered a bit. Leave it to Stacy and her down-home country accent to bring some form of amusement to an otherwise horrific situation.

"Amelia, this's my cousin, Stacy." She looked at her and offered a shy wave before looking back at me. "Amelia, we're gonna get out of here, all three of us, but to do that, we need your help."

"My help?" she asked, holding her hands close to her chest.

"Yeah, think for a second. At any moment, did you ever see a way out of this place?"

"A way out?"

"Yeah, like a... like an escape hatch or cellar door or something. Anything that could lead us outside?" She looked around for a moment, eyes narrowing at various random places in the room.

"I... I can't remember really..." She screwed up her face, grimacing.

"Fat lot of help..." Stacy remarked, scoffing.

"I-I'm sorry, I'm trying, just... I don't know." She frantically ran her hands through her hair.

"Shh, it's okay. Let's just get moving then. We'll figure this out together."

"Figure what out?" Stacy asked. "Oh, you mean navigating this hellhole blindly WITHOUT getting butchered?" She shot a look at Amelia, who shrank down because of this.

"Hey, come on now, that's enough. This isn't her fault, okay?"

"Isn't it?" she asked, snickering sarcastically. "For a third time, Cous, remind me just what the hell it is we're doing here anyway?"

"Trying to do something good, saving at least ONE person's life, okay? God knows I ain't good for much, but goddamn it, I'm not going out without doing ONE thing that makes this all worth it." The room drowned in silence after that. Stacy stood there, narrowing her eyes at me like she was caught between wanting to jump on her soapbox at me and rip me a new asshole, or concede yet another point. Amelia shrank down all the way to her knees and huddled them to her chest, watching this like she were watching her own parents arguing, not at all understanding what's being said or why.

The silence was broken by Stacy with an exhausted sort of sigh. "Roy, you know this isn't gonna bring her back." Her face had been switched from one of sarcastic snobbery to one of grim realism, like she were telling someone a loved one wasn't gonna make it. At least, that's how it hit with me, like she was telling me Bonnie was dead. The only difference is that there was no proof of this. She could still be out there, waiting to be found again.

"Who?" Amelia asked, poking her head up from her arms like a gopher. Her head swiveled back and forth between me and Stacy. Looking back at me, she timidly asked, "Who is she talking about, bring who back?" Stacy briefly darted her eyes back and forth from me to her and back to me.

"Nobody." I answered coldly, glaring at Stacy. The fuck was wrong with her, I wondered. That's a cheap shot, you know; using my little sister's kidnapping against me like that. The fuck?

Stacy sighed, pinching the bridge of her nose. "Look, you wanna get out of here, let's go. We'll talk later about who's got a point and who's just an ass, capisce?"

"Fine." I replied coldly. I looked back at Amelia. She'd started slowly to stand up again.

"So... what do we do?" she asked. Stacy began to take back up my left arm.

"We get the hell out of here, that's what." She started tugging on my arm, dragging it along behind her. "Alright, here's what we're gonna do. Amelia is it? I want you up front here with me, talking point, got me?" She looked at me, gauging me for some sort of response to this; perhaps an objection or something. Instead, I just nodded my head over to where Stacy was standing.

She went over to Stacy while she took my arms up again. "Alright, lead the way." she ordered. Amelia turned and began heading down the hallway. Stacy took to dragging me along again, straining almost the entire time. She managed to make it to about the halfway point in the next room before having to stop again. She caught her breath and took up my arms again and heaved. This little process ended up repeating for the next five or so rooms. It was in the last one that the stop lasted longer than half a minute like the other rooms. She slumped to the floor, breathless.

"I think we might be approaching the exit." Amelia piped up.

"You think?" Stacy scoffed. Amelia shrank into her shoulders again. "Look, Roy, I know you can't help it, but I can't keep lugging your ass around forever here. There's gotta be some way to tow you along, like a sheet or hell, a wagon to put you on. That'd be great right about now."

She looked at Amelia and sarcastically asked if there was a wagon somewhere around here.

"Um... Well..." She turned to the right, scratching her chin.

"It's fine, I was just--"

"Wait here, I'll be right back!" she exclaimed before turning and speed walking out into the hallway ahead of us.

"Hold on, where're you--, aaand she's gone. Perfect." She let out an exasperated sigh followed with a dry chuckle. "We're never getting out of this place, are we?" She chuckled again, almost emotionless this time, robotic even.

"Stacy..." I said, reaching out to her.

"What, you gonna tell me everything's fine? You gonna try and tell me that shit's "fine" here?"

"Stacy please, I--"

"Stacy please I what? You tried to talk me out of this and this is now my fault, right?"

"That's not what I was about to say, Stacy."

"Oh you might as damn well. You tried to tell me this was a bad idea and I was the ambitious little bitch I've always been."

"And I'm still the gullible, impressionable little dipshit I was back in the day, aren't I?" This earned me at least a small parting at the corner of her mouth.

"Look, I guess I'm trying to say I'm... I'm..." she sighed again and croaked out, voice cracking, "That I'm sorry, okay?"

"For what?" She chuckled sarcastically.

"For what?" For all of this. For begging you to drive up here. For you ending up the way you are now. I am, I'm... I'm--" I held up my hand.

"Hey, that's enough, okay? You may have pushed me to come, Stacy, but I was the one with the idea in the first place, okay? You didn't make me come up here, despite what I said, okay? And you were right, this wasn't me being noble or trying to "do the right thing" or any of that. This was for me. I just... I just... I couldn't bear to live, knowing that there was another little girl like Bonnie out there, missing, no one even looking for her. I just couldn't--"

"Shh..." I stopped, raising my eyebrow at her. Her eyes snapped around the room frantically.

"What? What's the--"

"Hush, you hear that?" I listened as hard as I could. I couldn't hear anything. I shook my head at her.

"What is it?"

"I... I don't know, it's like... like this..." She stopped abruptly, grimacing in pain.

"Stacy?" She arched over, clutching her ears. "Stacy, what's going on?"

"I... I don't... I can't... Fuck!" She doubled over more and more. Her head shook violently from side to side. "It hurts!" she screamed. My heart jackhammered. I couldn't move, but even if I could, I wouldn't have known what to do.

I attempted to reach out to her but she batted my hand away. "N-No, don't touch me! Stay away!" SHe scurried hurriedly away from my body.

"Stacy, talk to me, what's the matter?"

"I hear him squealing." She said, groaning. She cried out sharply.

"Squealing?"

"Yeah, like a pig." My eyes widened.

"What do you mean?"

"It's... Oh God, it's him!"

"Who?"

"Pig Man. I can hear him." She shrieked in pain before collapsing to a writhing ball on the floor a few feet away from me. "Get away! Leave me alone, augggh!"

"Stacy!" I began slugging along the floor again towards her. "Hang on, I'm coming!" I pulled myself along and had almost made it to her when I stopped, seeing her face look up at me. It was her face, but it wasn't her looking at me. Not anymore.

Her eyes were stitched wide, bloodshot and wild. "St-Stacy?" She didn't move. Her eyes were fixed on mine, glued to mine, examining me the way a dingo or a hyena examines a lone, stray wallaby in the desert. Her eyes were unintelligent, devoid of emotion, reason, or any common sense. They were the eyes of an animal.

Slowly, I tried pushing myself backward, back towards the door we'd come in from behind me. In an instant so sudden that I literally would've missed it if I'd blinked, She lunged at me, bounding through the air, landing right on top of me. The force of her body's impact straight onto my chest knocked the wind right out of me. The next thing I know, her fists are stoving my face more and more into the floor.

Not a single thought, coherent or otherwise, was allowed to stay in my head longer than a single second before being slugged out of me by my cousin. It was by the sixth or seventh blow that my sight exploded into nothing but fuzzy blobs of dark clouds around me. I couldn't see her face, but the image of her face from just seconds before filled that gap. Along with this, I could hear her squealing furiously, just like the kids were before.

Dear fucking Christ, she's become one of them!

She was relentless with her assault. If you'd seen her, you'd have thought I'd killed her dog or something. She was going to kill me, too, I could tell. Because of how much and how suddenly my brain was rattled, I couldn't even will myself to try bringing up my hands to block any of her blows either. It was just one fist after another, pounding my face harder and harder while she shrieked. My vision was close to going out completely when I felt her being forced off of me.

I craned my neck up. I couldn't really see either of them, but it sounded like Stacy was struggling with Amelia. I could hear the both of them wrestling with each other, rolling and slamming each other into the floor. My vision slowly came back to me, only to see that Stacy had Amelia pinned to the floor. I could only see Amelia's legs, but I could see them struggling frantically. I had to do something quick, else Amelia was going to be chow for my now deranged cousin.

Looking to my right, I managed to spot and grab ahold of a nearby can of beans that was on its side and threw it at her. It ended up bouncing off of her head and she fell off of Amelia. "Amelia." I called out. She slowly rose up to a sitting position from where she was.

"Amelia, are you ok--" I stopped, realizing she, too, was looking at me the same way Stacy was now. My body tensed and was about to at least try and dive out of the way for when she sprang for the kill when the door burst open and that terrifying bellow squeal from earlier blasted me right in my face. The breath of the beast alone was a hurricane blowing in my face.

My eyes opened and there he stood, the beast of the mountains, the haunter of my hometown and the embodiment of my childhood night terrors; Pig Man. He stood easily 8' tall, possibly 8 foot three or four. I would've been lucky to have even come up to chest level with this thing -- and I'm (well, was) at least 6' 2". Its dead, smoke black eyes beat down heavily on me, as though they were rocks bearing down on my chest. My heartbeat froze dead just looking into its eyes.

Amelia, I saw, was getting ready to pounce when Pig Man snorted from behind her, I guess signaling for her to stop. She went still and Pig Man took a lumbering stomp forward. The entire foundation of the house or whatever place this was shook as soon as his hoof touched the ground. I couldn't force myself to move, no matter how much I screamed at myself to do so. Another stomp forward sent the place quivering again, this time snatching my breath right out my chest.

Time at this point stood almost completely still. Reality -- or what I feared was reality and not just my single most twisted and vivid nightmare -- was tracking like a VCR at the slowest possible rate. Seconds were more like hours. Pig Man took one last earth-shaking stomp toward me, positioning himself just a hair's breadth away, like no more than two and a half feet at most. Despite what I said about time slowing to a crawl, it took less than a second for him to have me hoisted by my throat.

He held me about a foot, possibly two, off the floor, constricting his grip with each second that passed. Before I even knew it, I'd blacked out for... well God only knew which time that night. Unconscious though I was, I could still hear echoing squeals swirling around me. They were everywhere, sounding like they were coming from each and every kid from before. Their collective voices seemed to merge, creating this weird dissonance around me. They drew closer and closer to me, it seemed.

There was no dream or anything attached to these sounds, either. Only the squeals. Thousands upon thousands of squeals.

It was only another moment or so (relatively speaking anyway) before I "woke up" again. I say "wake up", but looking back, I'm starting to think I wasn't really asleep, not in the regular sense anyway. What I mean by this is that it seems like that occasion, as well as the first time I'd woke back up after the kids ambushed us on the pass, that I had visions or heard things that pertained all too well with the current situation and what I'd wake up to. Like before, I dreamt that Pig Man was about to eat me and what do I find when I wake up; my leg's gone.

The real driver of this point though is what happened when I woke up this time. My eyes opened to find that I was staring straight up at the moon. It shone down onto me with a full, pale ray of light that was obscured about halfway to me by at least a hundred shadows surrounding me, with one behemoth in the center whose shadow dominated most of the surrounding area, blanketing me and most of the ground in darkness. My neck arched upwards and there, once again, stood Pig Man, leering down at me. I heard him snort; a sickening sound in of itself that had my stomach turning over on itself. I could hear small grunting coming from all around me.

My eyes darted around to find the kids, all of them, all together, standing along a circle around me. They stood motionless, primed and ready to pounce the instant I attempted to make a move. Immediately, I found out just how unlikely it was though that I'd be able to do anything when I attempted to move my arms, only to find them tied down at various points in the circle. I looked down again, finding Pig Man's eyes boring harder and harder into me.

I could feel his breath blasting in my face. Hot, blistering almost. My heart and brain, at the same time, shut down. I couldn't think, I couldn't do anything, I couldn't move, Nothing. Just laid there, empty.

I realized this was it. This was the end. I'd slipped away, cheated death, and/or been rescued multiple times now, but that number was now up. I'd be just another missing person, never found again or if I am, it will be in so many different pieces that whoever finds them won't likely identify me. Just like the kid the cashier told me about. Just like the ones who'd come before him. Just like the ones my old man would always talk about. The ones he'd warn me about.

"I love you, son. Please, don't go chasing things that weren't meant to be chased."

Dad's words distantly echoed in my mind, devoured largely by the persistent ambience of the squealing but still enough for me to notice it. To feel it. Enough for it to really sink in that I'd broken my promise to Dad. I'd gone up the mountain, the forbidden mountain, searching for the truth of Pig Man. In doing this, I've now doomed not only myself, but both my own family and the one person who I'd come up for. And now, I was going to pay dearly for my disobedience.

And you wanna know what? I didn't care one single bit. About any of it. None of it mattered to me anymore. Not Amelia, not Stacy, not any of the other kids, and not even my promise to Dad. I didn't even care about making it off the mountain myself. "Numb", I guess you could call me. It'd be fitting, too, considering how I actually started losing feeling in my wrists -- though if I'm honest, I figure that's more thanks to the ropes binding my hands starting to cut off my circulation. I laid there, staring hollowly at

Pig Man, just waiting for whatever was going to happen to just happen already.

He stomped forward. I wasn't phased by it at all like I was before though. What felt before like an earthquake, now felt more akin to a small shaking now. Arching his bulging, flabby neck back, Pig Man raised up and blasted the night sky with a furious squeal. Still, I felt nothing.

The Earth quivered when the monster lumbered two more steps towards me. The kids drew closer to the circle as well. In their hands, they all held small candles except for one; one who, by her height, I could tell wasn't a child. I could hear her snorting through a pink paper plate mask of her own.

Stacy... Oh God...

Focusing my attention back on Pig Man, I realized he was wielding a giant ass ax. I couldn't help but actually start to laugh at this. There it all was, yet again, the same damn thing I saw in my nightmare except this time, I knew good and damn well this wasn't a dream. I was wide awake, for the last time, it would seem.

The crowd raised their torches and squealed, prompting Pig Man to do the same, raising his ax to the sky. The whole area -- which by the way, appeared to be a large, oversized sort of patio deck or some sort of deck around the back of the house I was in before -- was one great big cage of rabid, deranged animals. By this point, believe it or not, I wasn't bothered by any of it, even from Pig Man himself. That said, I still seize up at the slightest noise resemblance to their squeals I hear anywhere here at home.

Finally, the place quieted down a bit again and all eyes were focused on me again. The ax raised high in the air before coming down. like how it was earlier, time went into a snail's crawl. What should've ended in five seconds or less, ended up feeling more like five minutes. Perhaps it's because of this that I was actually granted a moment to think of a possible way out of this situation.

I'll say it right now, adrenaline has got to be one of the most powerful forces on this fucking planet because what I did next was done from adrenaline and instinct alone. Right before the ax could come down, slicing my right arm, I managed to jerk it upward so hard that the rope holding me was actually caught by the blade instead. My hand was free, and when the ax was raised again, I rolled over onto the other arm. The ground shook again when the ax embedded itself into the ground.

I frantically started fumbling with the other wrist while Pig Man was recovering the ax. The crowd was in an uproar at this, shrieking and squealing louder and more furiously than ever. I heard the ax head unsheath from the ground before feeling it shake beneath me again with his stomping. Whoever among the kids that tied me up, though, knew exactly what they were doing because no matter how much I pried and picked at it, even tearing through some of the skin under the rope, that bitch wasn't coming undone.

I picked and picked until I heard the stomping behind me cease and the beast's gigantic shadow blanketed me. Just like it was a second ago, adrenaline alone caused me to roll out of the way yet again when I saw his massive arm raise the ax in the air, ready to bring it down straight on top of my head. Luck hadn't run out on me yet, either, because sure enough, the ax came down and I found my other hand freed. Now came the hard part; how to get out of this without the use of my legs or anyone to help me along.

If you're about to ask me how I did get out of this situation, well... I guess the short answer is luck. Pure, simple, dumbass luck. At least, from a purely pragmatic point of view anyway.

As soon as my other wrist was free, I took to rolling on my side. Pathetic and given the current environment and circumstances, doomed to fail miserably, but who the hell cared about that? I was free and there was a reawakened sense of urgency, a resurgent will to fight, to stay alive. And up to that point, rolling had seemed to work.

I made it to one of the edges of the deck and that was when the kids decided to finally jump in. In less than a second, I had five of them smothering me while about six or seven others started kicking, scratching, and even biting at me everywhere else. I flailed and thrashed around as hard as I possibly could, but just like every other time I tried this, tried fighting these kids off of me, it did absolutely no good. The ground shook harder and faster as Pig Man came barreling up to where I was. Underneath the kids, I just barely saw the giant ax raise into the air and swing down.

When it did, instead of crushing me, it skewered at least three of the five on top of me, sending them flying across the deck when he withdrew and raised up for another crack. Two more kids ended up taking the place of the former, only to immediately meet the same fate as them. This happened one more time, with two more trying to gnash at my face and getting split in half by Pig Man's ax. That's when I saw something; both an opportunity as well as a lifelong nightmare.

The kids, despite seeing what was happening to the others that kept trying to come for me, they were unhinged, feral, wanting nothing but to stuff their little cheeks with flesh. Not just my flesh either apparently. I began watching two of them start violently clawing at each other, ripping bigger and bigger chunks out of each other relentlessly. I could faintly see the way they were looking at each other while they did this, too. They weren't doing it out of anger, out of malice, no, they were just doing it, just eating each other. No rhyme, reason, or conscience, just mindless brutality.

It wasn't long before the rest of them followed suit and soon, the entire deck was nothing but on great big slaughtering ground. No friends or enemies, just animals doing what animals do, eat each other. Pig Man roared, I guess trying to maybe redirect their attention back to me or silence them, one, but it was no good anymore. Whatever control he might've had, whatever sort of leash he had them on, was gone. Eventually, the ones on top of me clamored off of me and set their sights on the much bigger meal in front of them.

In no particular order or pattern, I watched the kids hurl themselves at the monster. Many of them were batted away by the swing of his ax, but a number of them still managed to find themselves latched onto their swine master, gnawing and tearing away at him as they had been with me. Soon, they were all over him, holding on for dear life while Pig Man himself roared, stomped, and flailed furiously.

He staggered all around the deck, trying desperately to shake them off, to no avail. He took to rolling on the ground, flattening many of them into nothing but a giant red stain on the deck. Others, I saw him even snatch up and either batter their heads into the ground or even hurl into that big gaping mouth of his, devouring them whole. All of this, and yet the little bastards just kept coming -- the ones that weren't either tearing each other apart or tearing chunks out of themselves (Yes, they actually ate themselves, some of them anyways)!

In any other circumstance, I probably would've been frozen where I was, too frightened, confused, mindfucked, as well as just too damn exhausted, physically and mentally, to move or do anything. This wasn't a normal circumstance, though. I saw this right then for what it was, one last chance at getting out of this worse-than-Hell on earth place, and you best believe I took it.

In a heartbeat, I took to rolling off the edge of the deck, which I found led down a very steep, very rocky decline down a few feet of the mountain, leading to a stretch of the road the house was overlooking. Before I'd hit the road, though, I hit my head pretty hard on one of the bumpier rocks on the way down, instantly knocking me out. This was the only time since all of this, that I'd actually gotten real sleep after blacking out. By this, I mean that there were no dreams, no illusions, no sort of telepathic shit from Pig Man, nothing. Just silent rest.

Well, okay "rest" might be overshooting a bit, but the point still stands that this was the first time I didn't wake up after a vivid nightmare, and then find that it wasn't even a nightmare at all. No, this time, I didn't wake up until well into the next afternoon, when I was being shaken awake. I awoke to find a middle aged man standing over me.

"You alright there, son?" asked the man. I didn't answer. There was only one thought present in my mind at that moment, was I finally free and clear of Pig Man and those kids? Were they after me now, after narrowly escaping from whatever their little ritual was on the deck? If not, what could I do, and if so, what was I gonna do now?

"Hey, there, looks like you've had a real rough one, haven't you?" he asked, finally grabbing my attention fully. "Jesus, what've you been getting into, huh? Christ, your damn leg's missin'!" He looked up at me, horrified, and asked what the hell happened. I responded simply by looking back up at the mountain. I should mention that my sight was shot all to hell, thanks to the crack on the old noggin', rendering everything to be little more than just a brightly colored cloud.

"Unh... Wh-Where am I?" I heard the guy laugh. It was then that I realized exactly who this was, too. This was the cashier from the gas station.

"You're in the middle of the mountain pass, and since I answered your question, maybe you can do the same for

me and tell me just how and what the hell you're doin'
here 'cause I just about mistook ya for roadkill." I groaned,
attempting to sit up, only to fall right back on my back
again. He laughed again.

"Hold on, there, take it easy. Here." I felt him take up
my arm and try helping me up. My body essentially was
dead weight at that point though, so it wasn't long before
he gave that up and opted to just lift me straight up and
into his truck. After that, he started driving down the
mountain pass again. About five or so minutes in, my
vision begins to fade more and more while my mind starts
to get cloudy. I couldn't tell whether I was about to pass
out for the millionth time or if this was finally going to be
it, I was finally going to kill over, right there in this guy's
truck.

My eyes closed, but I wasn't quite out yet. Faintly, I
heard him ask me, "So I'm just gonna go out on a limb
here and say that you decided not to take my advice,
right?" I groaned. It felt like my brain was in a blender
after waking up. You know how in the morning when you
first wake up, your brain's not all there? Or more
appropriate for my case, when you just get out of an
extremely exhilarating moment and your brain is just
starting to settle back in? Everything's all fuzzy and shit,
right, not sure whether it wants you to fall asleep or stay

awake and you can't respond or really interact with anyone, comprehend anything, or even move.

That's what this was for me, anyways. Couldn't see, couldn't think, couldn't move. I was dead weight in this guy's truck.

We stopped sometime after and he carried me out. I briefly opened my eyes to find myself entering the hospital just on the edge of my hometown. As soon as I was pushed through the threshold, I finally clocked out. I woke up again to find myself in an admittedly comfortable bed (for a hospital bed, anyways). To my right, the E.K.G. monitor beeped softly while the open window at my left kept me just cool enough under the thick, heavy blankets I was under. I looked down toward the foot of the bed and found my right foot, "ol' stumpy" as Stacy would've said, mummified in bandages while the other one dangled limply in a sling.

A minute or two later, the door opened and in stepped both a doctor and a police officer. By this time, my head had already rested well and wasn't cloudy anymore, though whether this was a good thing or not, with the cop there, was debatable for me. My stomach clenched up. Lucid or not, I was in absolutely no mind for anyone, cop or not, to be poking and prodding me for questions about the mountain. I wanted one thing and one thing only, and that was to leave this town and never come back. The doctor started changing my bandages while the police officer began questioning me.

"Look, son, I can see you've had a rough time, and frankly, I ain't trying to make things hard for either of us, so just answer me these few questions and I'll leave you alone. That sound good to you?"

"Yeah, uh... Yeah, sure, I guess."

"Good. First, I need to know, you from around here?"

"No. Well, not anymore. I grew up here, but I live in Massachusetts, attending the university there." He chuckled.

"College boy, huh?" I nodded. "Okay, next question, since it's clear you had went up the mountain, and was found face down in the road, I have to ask, what exactly were you--"

"Amelia Hill, sir." I blurted. His eyebrows cocked at me.

"Huh? Who's that? Someone you know?" I shook my head. I went to try pulling the missing poster for her out of my pocket but found that my arms were little more than wet noodles attached to my body.

I sighed and said, "She was a recent missing person who'd gone up there. I found the poster and... well..." I trailed off. This was of course the part of this conversation that I was dreading; the part where I had to admit that my dumb ass had gone and dragged both myself and my cousin up the mountain just to play hero, all just to get royally screwed in every nightmarish way possible.

Fortunately, he seemed to get the point, even if said point ended up earning me the "Really dude?" look. He sighed and jotted notes in his little notepad while I laid patiently waiting for the next humiliating question. "So here's my last question. Given that you're the only person in YEARS who's managed to come back from the mountain alive, I need to ask, what all exactly did you see up there?"

And there it was, the one single, biggest question I feared most of all that'd come. I looked at him, giving him the look that said without saying "I REALLY don't want to". He stood waiting anyway. I sighed, trying to figure out exactly what the hell I was supposed to say. I wasn't real sure he'd believe me, bit then again, who's to say he wouldn't either? I mean, he would've heard the legends, given the way he'd responded to me telling him about going up the mountain. Thing is, what would happen if I did admit the truth?

Not knowing of any alternative, I sucked down my anxiety and answered, "I saw the truth, sir. I saw exactly what happens to the people that go missing on the mountain. I saw them all eating each other."

"Them?" he asked, raising his eyebrow.

"The children. The missing children. All of them, eating each other."

"You mean the kids ran away to the mountain and--"

"No. They were taken."

"By?"

"Pig Man. He's real. I don't know how, but he's real, and he uses those kids to bring others back as either food or as another pledge."

"How? How is he driving the kids to do these things?"

"I... I'm not real sure, okay? I didn't ever catch it, but I know that he had some sort of psychic hold over them."

"You mean Pig Man was mind controlling them?"

"Sort of. It was more like a drive into madness."

"How so?"

"Well, the only reason I escaped was because they all turned on each other. They'd all swarmed Pig Man while ripping each other apart." For just a second, I paused, faintly hearing the multitude of agonizing squeals filling the night sky to the brim.

"So you think they're all dead up there?" he asked. What I said next is something I regret just as much, if not even a bit more so, as when I let Stacy talk me into going up the mountain in the first place, "Maybe." He clicked his pen and thanked me for my time before leaving the room.

I have to end this here. I can't tell you how hard it's been to write this, having to relive every minute of the worst days of my life like this. I wouldn't have done it all, had I not found the news article online, talking about sending a police unit to scour the mountain for any survivors. They were going up the mountain, looking for Pig Man, just like I had!

Look, I'd already let so many down; Stacy, Dad, Amelia and all the other missing kids for that matter... Bonnie... But goddamn it, I'm not going to have blood from any more people staining my hands because of that mountain. I suffered a lifetime of torment in just a few hours just so no one else would have to, and so I've written this here for emphasis.

Sometimes, we are told strange things when we are young and we might not understand why. But believe me when I say that there is a reason, and sometimes, that reason is far too strange and horrific to explain. Either way, though, the point still stands, there is truth to warnings, and should you decline to heed them, you may well find it costing you dearly. Sometimes the truth is better left alone; truths, such as the legend of Pig Man.

<u>Words from the author</u>

Greetings from the Underdark. Here we are again, my friends. This story, I want to emphasize, is one that strikes more than one cord for me. As a kid, I used to be told many times of the tale of "Pig Man", mainly by my late stepfather.

As I understand, it was a legend passed around by him and his friends back in Boy Scouts when he was much younger. I remember how fascinated by it I always used to be. I remember asking him, "Can he be killed by anything", to which he'd reply "You'd have to catch him first."

Mainly, though, as vivid and surreal an imagination as I possess, especially from back in that time, I had believed him when he'd tell me of "Pig Man". Over time, of course, I had lost a lot of my fascination with the supposed existence of him, but I never stopped believing in it, either. Right up until the point he told me straight up that no, "Pig Man" wasn't real, I believed that he did.

Something my stepfather always believed in, whether it be a joke, a funny story, or even a campfire legend like this one, he always believed in the art of delivery. He and I often didn't see eye to eye on many things, but even a macabre scribe like myself can't deny, the man knew how to deliver a story.

I say all of this to say, essentially, that along with my family and, of course all of you; my beloved maggots and larvae, this volume is dedicated to my stepfather, David Elliott. Given that he is no longer with us, we (myself included) can only wonder what he would've thought of his tale being brought to life like this. I'd like to think he'd be proud.

But I must obviously thank you all for your continued support of my work. Without you all, all who've listened to the various audio adaptations of my work, subscribed to my subreddit community, R/CorpseChildGospels, or even those who've gone the full mile and subscribed to the Sanctuary online and signed up for my monthly newsletters, I very likely would've lost much of my motivation to continue in my craft. I will always be a horror author, but without you, I would just be another unknown scribe, lost to his own madness.

Thank you for helping me to not have to linger in the madness completely alone.

And thank you, David, for your delivery of the legends of "Pig Man". God rest, buddy.

Call to action

If you have not already, beloved maggots and larvae, please join me in the Sanctuary by going to www.corpsechildssanctuary.com, sign up for updates on what happens here in the dark each month, as well as brand new, fresh, original gospels of dread released every Sunday morning to start your week with a chill, and "Monster Beat Down" every Friday night where you get to decide which of your favorite iconic movie monsters get to live on, and which shall be forever buried like the ghouls of old!

If you'd like as well, follow me on TikTok at @unholy_corpse_child, where I'm always announcing new deals or just fun little things about my work.

About the Author

Thomas Stewart is 22 years old with a fascination with the art of terror and the macabre. When he's not watching horror movies, or reading horror novels or stories, he's always crafting his own chilling gospels of horror to terrify and eternally rob you of a peaceful slumber. Currently he publishes most his work to Reddit under his pen name "Corpse Child". Many of his horror stories have been featured and adapted to audio narrations by a wide variety of YouTube narrators — including some of the bigger names in the field — as well as the ones commissioned on the ChillingApp and was featured in the debut issue of IllAdvised Records' "The Dark Door" E-zine and has recently published his debut horror novella.

You can follow him for more of his work through his Facebook and his SubReddit; "r/CorpseChildGospels" or his website; "Corpse Child's Sanctuary" as well as purchasing a copy of his books, "Damned Whispers" and "The Other Side" on Amazon, as well as his debut horror novella, "Mortimer".

F.B. — https://www.facebook.com/profile.php?id=100089381 146632&mibextid=LQQJ4d

Thomas Stewart

Subreddit:
www.reddit.com/r/CorpseChildGospels/

Website: www.corpsechildssanctuary.com